Pup Fiction™
Adventure Series
by
LaMonte Heflick

The Story of Fat Cat

The Story of Big Dog

The Story of Sweet the Skunk

The Story of Ninja Cat

The Story of Pup Daddy

The Story of Boney and Clyde

About the Author

LaMonte Heflick is a speech-language-hearing pathologist with the Elkhart Community Schools in Elkhart, Indiana. Mr. Heflick also teaches Chinese and Japanese at North Side, Pierre Moran, and West Side Middle Schools. In addition to his SLP license, Mr. Heflick is certified in Learning Disabilities, Teaching English to Speakers of Other Languages (TESOL), Japanese, and Mandarin Chinese.

The Story of Pup Daddy

by LaMonte Heflick

Illustrated by John Lakey

Remedia Publications
Scottsdale, Arizona

Title: The Story of Pup Daddy
ISBN# 1-56175-902-3

Published by:
Remedia Publications, Inc.
15887 N. 76th St. #120
Scottsdale, Arizona 85260
www.rempub.com

Cover Design by Don Merrifield

I Am A Dog

I am a dog. I am my **own** dog.

I used to live with some people. But that was when I was just a pup.

The kid in the family used to call me *puppy dog.*

But sometimes after a cute little puppy grows up … it ain't so cute anymore. That's what happened to me.

I grew up. The kid grew up. They got tired of me.

One day when the kid was away at summer camp, his parents threw me out. I think they told the kid that I got run over by a truck or hit by a car or something like that.

But don't get me wrong. I'm not asking for pity. I'm not crying about it. I'm just telling you the truth. I'm just telling you the facts. Anyway, I'm on my own now. My friends call me Pup Daddy.

I Was Lucky

Yes, I'm on my own now. And it was bad … at first. I didn't know where to go. I didn't know where to eat. I didn't know where to sleep.

But a hard life, if you survive long enough, can make you strong.

You can rise above it. You can be a winner.

And I had a lucky break.

I grew up listening to music. All the time there was music. Jazz music.

Good jazz music. At first I used to howl about it. But then I got used to it. And then I started liking it.

Well, when I got pushed out on the street, I met a jazz cat who could really play the saxophone. He was the best sax player that I ever heard.

He took me in. He gave me a place to sleep. He gave me something to eat. And he kept me out of trouble.

He Gave Me My Start

My friend's name is Cool Cat.

He is not a regular street cat. This guy has class.

His father was just an old tom cat but his mother was Siamese. She was a pure breed of Siamese, good stock, 100%.

His mother got him started on the piano at the age of 2. He was a real *kitten on the keys*. Then at the age of 3, he took lessons on the sax.

One day, he let me try his sax.

Wah! Wah! Waaaaaaah! Wah!
He said I was a **natural**. I was
playing songs by ear right from the
start.

I guess it's because I heard so much
good jazz as a pup. The tunes were
floating around in my head. All I
had to do was hit the right notes. It
was cool!

So this is where the story really
begins.

I play sax with Cool Cat at his club.
He gave me a start.

The Hot Club

"The place is jumping tonight!"

"It sure is," said Milton. "And Cool Cat is hot! Just listen to that cat play!"

"Thank you, thank you," said Cool Cat. "You're too kind. Now ladies and gentle-cats, I'd like to introduce you to a good friend of mine. This is only his first week at the Hot Club. Please put your paws together and make welcome ... Pup Daddy!"

Pup Daddy started his set with a ballad—a slow, sweet tune—*You Don't Know How It Feels*. The place got quiet. The crowd loved it.

And so did a young, lovely film actress from Hollywood. She sipped her milk-o-lotta and gazed longingly through big, round, emerald green eyes. Looking over the rim of her glass, she smiled at Pup Daddy.

Too Cool

The band went into a swing number. Cool Cat and Pup Daddy had the place rocking. Everyone was on their feet.

At 11:00 p.m., the band took a break. As Pup Daddy walked off stage, Milton handed him a note written on a napkin.

The note said:

Mr. Pup Daddy, May I buy you a drink? I like your style.—Grrrrrr!

Pup Daddy looked around.

"It's from the tall Afghan," said Milton. "She's in that back booth." He pointed. "Over there."

"Thanks, Milton," said Pup Daddy.

"Be cool," added Milton. "She's big-time Hollywood."

Miss Julia

Pup Daddy walked to the back booth. "Bow Wow! Miss …?"

"Julia," she said, as she extended her cream-colored paw. "Julia Afghan." She put her arm on the back of a chair. "Here," she smiled. "Have a seat."

"Thank you," said Pup Daddy. "Is it Miss or Missus?" he asked.

"It's **Miss** Julia Afghan," she smiled. "I do like the way you blow that horn."

13

"Are you alone?" asked Pup Daddy.

"I can be," she said with a wink.

Pup Daddy's cheeks turned a soft pink-red.

"Irish, aren't you?" she asked.

"Yes, Irish Setter, Miss Julia," said Pup Daddy. "A mix, actually," he added. "My mother was part Airedale."

Greyhound

Just then a tall, thin, grey-haired greyhound walked up to the table. He wore a gold collar.

"Sorry I'm late, babe," he said to Miss Julia.

"This is Flash," said Miss Julia.

"Flash," said Julia, "I'd like you to meet Pup Daddy. He plays with the band."

"Oh!" said Flash. "Do you bang on the pots and pans?" he asked as he wrinkled his forehead.

"No, I'm not a drummer," said Pup Daddy. "I play sax."

"Yes," smiled Julia. "He's the best young musician I've ever heard."

"I'm just a beginner, Miss Julia," said Pup Daddy. "And I owe it all to Cool Cat. He took me in."

"Got you off the streets, did he? Out of the alley?" asked Flash, looking down his long, narrow nose.

With A Silver Spoon

"Yes, he did," said Pup Daddy, looking directly at Flash. "Cool Cat got me off the streets." There was a slight tone of anger in his voice. "We can't all be born into a nice home ... with a silver spoon in our mouths," he continued.

"Flash was a racing dog," said Julia. "He retired. Now he's my manager."

"I see," said Pup Daddy. "Is he your manager ... or your **owner**?" he asked.

"Manager," replied Julia without hesitation.

"Well, I have to get back to work," said Pup Daddy. "This is the dance set coming up. Nice to meet you."

"Nice to meet you, too," said Miss Julia with a big smile.

"Yeah, sure," grunted Flash. "Break a leg."

"Be cool," said Pup Daddy. He moved back to the stage and picked up his sax. "Let's rock this place!"

Old Dog

Pup Daddy stepped onto the stage.
He was excited.

"A nice-looking girl," said Cool Cat.
"And it's easy to see that she likes
you."

"Yes, she is," said Pup Daddy.
"She sure looks nice."

"And what's not to like?" Pup
Daddy joked.

"But that greyhound has his dog tag
around her neck."

The band started off with a real hot tune—*"Jump Back Doggy, Jump Back, Don't Bite Doggy, Don't Bite."*

Miss Julia stood up and took Flash's paw.

"Come on," she said. "Let's dance."

Flash pulled back. "It's getting late, we should go. We have a busy day ahead of us."

"Don't be such an **old** dog," insisted Julia. "Let's dance."

Maybe it was the way she said "old". Because Flash went out the door. "Walk home," he snarled.

Shall We Dance?

The music was hot. The band was jammin'. The walls were shaking. Everybody was dancing.

Miss Julia wanted to dance too. So she danced by herself. Right in front of the stage. She was dancing right in front of the sax player. And Pup Daddy was loving it.

For an hour and 30 minutes the band kept the place hopping.

Then, Cool Cat stepped up to the microphone and sang:

"Puppy love, no this ain't just puppy love.
I'm a fool for you, this ain't just puppy love ..."

Miss Julia felt a light touch—a paw on the middle of her back. She turned around.

"Shall we dance?" asked Pup Daddy.

Miss Julia looked up at him. She smiled and moved closer. "I'd love to."

But I'll Write

Julia put her head on Pup Daddy's shoulder. They danced as Cool Cat sang. The night became a special night for the young couple.

Cool Cat finished the song. Then he led the band in a be-bop jazz song.

"Shall we sit a bit?" Miss Julia took Pup Daddy's paw.

"Sure," said Pup Daddy. He followed her to the table.

They ordered a couple of Beef Broth Sodas ... on the rocks.

"I'd like to get to know you better," began Julia. Her dark, emerald green eyes got bigger and bigger. "But I have to get back to Hollywood. We start shooting a new picture on Monday. But I'll write."

"Please do," said Pup Daddy. "I'd like that a lot." He sniffed the air. "But what about Flash?"

"Flash is my manager, not my boyfriend and not my daddy."

Something On His Mind

Pup Daddy never had trouble sleeping at night. But that was before he met Miss Julia. Now he had something on his mind. He had a problem. A big problem. He was *in love.*

Cool Cat smiled. "Boy," he said to Pup Daddy, "you are in big trouble."

Pup Daddy looked at the floor.

"I bet you'll be playing that sax with feeling tonight."

Pup Daddy's tail was swinging side-to-side.

"Yes, Pup Daddy, you have got it bad." Cool Cat smiled real big. "Now don't get me wrong ... it feels good. Being in love sure feels good, but it hurts, too."

Pup Daddy was all ears. He didn't say a word.

"And your honey is a long way off ... in Hollywood."

The First Letter

The first letter arrived 3 days later.

The letter said:

Dear Pup Daddy,

I had a wonderful time at the Hot Club.

Your band is so much fun! And you play so well!

We started filming a new movie yesterday.

So, I'll be very busy for the next month and a half. But I hope to get back to Chicago in September. May I see you then?

I miss you!

Julia

Pup Daddy gave a loud howl. His hind foot thumped the floor. *Hoooooooooooowwwwwwwwl!* "Did you hear that," he said to himself. "She's coming back to Chicago in September!"

That night, the club was packed. The place was rocking. Pup Daddy played the best set of his life. *Wah! Waah!* He was on fire! *Wah! Waaaaaah! Waah! Waa! Wah! Wah!*

More Letters

The pups wrote more letters.
Everyday, more love letters …
until …

One day, Pup Daddy got a strange
letter.

The letter said:

> Hey! Dog meat!
> Stay away from my girl!
> And don't bother to write.
> She moved!

Flash!? thought Pup Daddy. *That old greyhound is jealous.*

Pup Daddy wrote to Miss Julia anyway.

But all the letters were returned ... unopened.

Pup Daddy was singing the blues and playing the blues.

The crowds still came into the club. The band still rocked the place. But Pup Daddy was down in the dumps. He was a lovesick puppy. A dog down on his luck.

September Came And Went

September came and went. The letters had stopped. There was no sign of Miss Julia.

Pup Daddy was okay. He was starting to get over her. Until one day as he was walking past a movie theater, he saw a large poster of Miss Julia.

It was an ad for her latest movie— *The Story of Al Catbone.*

He bought a ticket and went in.

The movie was not bad. But Miss Julia was wonderful.

He told Cool Cat that he wanted to go to California. He wanted to try to find her. He **had** to find her.

"You're dreaming," Cool Cat told him. "Get real. Get a grip. Get a life. Move on."

"Maybe she's in trouble," said Pup Daddy. "She might need me. She might need help."

Okay, But You'll Need Money

"Okay," said Cool Cat. "I guess there's no way to talk you out of it. Just go on. Go chasing around Hollywood. But you'll need money. And you'll need a job."

"I have money," said Pup Daddy. "Not much, but enough."

"Not the kind of money that you'll need in Hollywood." Cool Cat opened his saxophone case.

"Now listen, I have a friend in L.A.," said Cool Cat. "Maybe he can line you up with some work at his club. You'll be up against the big boys, so don't think for a moment that you'll be blowing your sax center stage. But it'll be work ... and you won't be out on the streets."

"Thanks, Cool Cat," said Pup Daddy. "You've always been like a father to me."

"Just keep your nose clean. Don't take any chances. L.A. is not Chicago. They got a different set of rules." Cool Cat adjusted the reed on his sax. "Go on out there ...

take your little look around. When you find out what you want to know … then, get your tail back home. Hear?"

California

It was Pup Daddy's first time on a jet plane. It was excitement that he was feeling, not fear. He kept his nose pressed to the window during takeoff. He was as nervous as a pup at the vet.

He played with the headphones. Rocked in his seat. Then he settled down and watched the in-flight movie. Guess what movie? It was *The Story of Al Catbone.*

He took a nap and dreamed of Miss Julia Afghan.

The plane landed in L.A. at 4:30 in the afternoon. He took a taxi to the Hot Dog Hotel.

He took a shower, brushed his teeth, and combed his hair and whiskers.

At 6:30, he had a bowl of puppy chow in a restaurant across the street from the hotel. He sat in a booth near the window. He watched the flow of people and animals on the sidewalk: a tall, blonde French Poodle, a big cat in an orange and yellow Hawaiian shirt, and a red fox wearing large, dark sunglasses and a beanie hat.

The Palm Tree

At 9:30 that evening, Pup Daddy took an uptown bus to the Palm Tree Club on Sunset Strip.

He walked in. The place was busy, but not crowded. It was still early. There was music from a jukebox.

"The band doesn't start until 10:30," said a snow white Maltese kitten as she walked from around the hostess counter. "Hi," she smiled. "May I help you?"

"I'm looking for Mr. Spats," said Pup Daddy as he brushed past a girl fox wearing a puffy, pink evening dress. "Pardon me," he whispered.

"May I ask who wants to see him?"

"Me ... me ..." stuttered Pup Daddy. "Just me ... I'm a friend of a friend of his ... Cool Cat. I'm looking for a job. I, uh ... I ... I play the saxophone."

He was usually pretty smooth. But tonight, he lost his cool. Maybe he was tired. It had been a long flight from Chicago. Or was he feeling out of place in L.A.?

I'll Have What
He's Having

The Maltese showed him to a lime-green booth in the corner. "Wait here," she told him. "It may be quite a while. Mr. Spats is a busy dog."

Then, she leaned closer to him. "Listen. Relax. I just came out to California myself 6 months ago. I'm an actress."

"An actress?" Pup Daddy stroked his right ear.

"Well, part-time," she said with a little giggle. "Can I get you something to drink while you're waiting?"

Pup Daddy pointed. "I'll have what he's having," he said.

"One Iced Shanghai Side Car coming right up!"

Pup Daddy stretched his legs out under the table. He heard a young, long-haired kitten at the next table say, "Look who just came in. It's Roverstein, the producer." A tall, slightly overweight, jet black Bombay cat walked in. He wore a fox fur coat and a white Panama hat. A purple scarf was tied loosely around his neck.

The Band Played On

At 10:35, the lights grew dim. A thin, middle-aged collie walked out on stage. "Bow Wow!" he said. He raised his paws above his head. "The Palm Tree Club is proud to present Tommy Ray's Big Time Big Band."

The crowd gave a modest round of applause.

On stage, a heavy red curtain was raised to the ceiling.

A 16-piece orchestra jumped into Glenn Miller's swing tune—*In The Mood.*

Nobody danced.

The band became background music for a hundred different conversations.

Around 11:15, the friendly Maltese came back. "Sorry you had to wait so long. Would you like to see a menu?"

"No thanks, just a salad and coffee ... black, please." Pup Daddy was beginning to have second thoughts.

Where Are You From?

It was 11:30. And still no sign of Mr. Spats. The big red curtain came down. The band took a 15-minute break.

The Maltese came back to check on Pup Daddy. "So ..." she said, feeling sorry for him, "where are you from?"

"The midwest ... Chicago."

"You're kidding!" she exclaimed, with her pretty white teeth showing. "I'm from Gary. In Indiana."

48

"It's a small world, isn't it?"

The Maltese put out her paw. "My name's Ling Ling." Then she added, "It's really June ... June Ling. But out here, I go by Ling Ling. Pleased to meet you."

Pup Daddy took her paw. It was warm. He smiled. He felt comfortable for the first time since he had arrived in California. He held her paw for a full minute.

"I'll get you another cup of coffee." As she walked, she looked back over her shoulder at Pup Daddy.

The Show Starts

The band played a short introduction as Miss Barbara Straystrand strolled to center stage.

Everyone got to their feet. Thunderous applause filled the room.

Although much older now, Miss Straystrand is still one of the best singers of her time. And deserving of the highest respect.

June came back with a hot cup of black coffee. "Sorry, it looks like you won't get to see Mr. Spats. He just left."

"He just left?" said Pup Daddy. "You're kidding."

"No," said June, "I'm afraid not. Business, I guess."

"I'm not broke," said Pup Daddy. "But I need a job." He drew circles on the table with his paw. "I'm looking for a friend," he continued. "And I'm planning on staying in town until I find her."

Maybe I Can Help

"Maybe I can help," said June, with a hurt look. "Who are you looking for? Your sister?"

"No," said Pup Daddy. "A friend of mine ... Miss Julia Afghan."

"You mean **the** Miss Julia Afghan? The actress!?"

"Yes, I met her in Chicago. And she was writing to me ... until ... until ... I don't know what happened."

"I hope you're not hot on her or nothing," frowned June. "She comes in here two or three times a month."

"She does?" Pup Daddy's eyes opened wide.

"She sure does," continued June. "And she doesn't look lonely, if you know what I mean."

"Stop in tomorrow," said June as she wiped the table. "It's a little easier to catch Mr. Spats on a Saturday. And if you're lucky, you might run into Miss Afghan."

She Walked
Right Past Me

The next evening, Pup Daddy got to the club early.

"Back again," said June. "Mr. Spats just stepped out."

But Pup Daddy was more interested in looking for Miss Julia. His eyes scanned the tables and the dance floor.

By 11:30 the place had filled up. All the beautiful people, rich dogs, and painted cats were out tonight. The dance floor was jammed. Everyone was dancing.

Pup Daddy was on his way to the Dog's Room when he saw Miss Julia. She had just arrived. And she was coming in the door. She walked in his direction. As they passed, their eyes met. Pup Daddy's pulse shot up. His heart raced. But ... nothing.

Nothing? No response, no reaction, no thanks, amigo? thought Pup Daddy, as he returned to his seat.

He pulled himself together. He pulled hard on his right ear. Then he stood up. He went over to her table. "Miss Julia," he said. "How nice to see you again."

Back In Chicago

one month later, at the Hot Club in Chicago

"Great job!" said Cool Cat. "Pup Daddy, you're hot tonight. Let's take a break. Want to join us?"

"I'll be there in a minute," said Pup Daddy. "But first, I see a friend in the audience."

Pup Daddy walked towards a table in the middle of the room. He was greeted with open arms and a warm, loving smile. The girl cat was not drop-dead beautiful, but she was very pretty. Her long hair flowed down over her shoulders. Her teeth were bright white. She gave Pup Daddy a "hi-hello-there-sweet-baby kiss".

Pup Daddy put his arms around her. A big smile. A big hug. He held her close a long time. "Come on. I want to introduce you to someone."

"Cool Cat," he said. "This is my fiancée, Miss June Ling."

"So happy to meet you, June," said Cool Cat. "I've heard so much about you. Please join us. What can I get you?"